Little Trouble in Tall Tree

A Baby Noir™ Mystery

by Michael Fertik

Little Trouble in Tall Tree

A Baby Noir™ Mystery

Little Trouble in Tall Tree
A Baby Noir™ Mystery

by Michael Fertik

ISBN 978-0-9884131-0-8

A Baby Noir™ Mystery is a registered
trademark of Tall Tree Enterprises, llc

PR by Julia Drake PR
Illustrations by Jamie Stroud
Creative Direction & Design by Angela Stout
Published by Tall Tree Enterprises, llc

For the real Squeezy

LITTLE TROUBLE IN TALL TREE

CHAPTER ONE

"Call me Squeezy."

Call him Squeezy. A dangerous proposition from what I'd heard, but you never know in this business. Maybe it was a sign of affection and the rumors were all bad formula. No matter what, I had to stay on top of my game. Squeezy the Cheeks was, rumor or no, the most volatile and wily baby gangster in the entire North Wood section of Tall Tree.

I raised my arms in an involuntary overhead stretch. I think he took it to mean I hadn't quite heard him. That happens a lot with baby gangsters.

"Yeah, call me Squeezy," he said again. His mouth dribbled, but I don't think he noticed.

"Okay, I will. Thank you."

"And what do I call you? The new kid."

"I don't know. I'm fresh out. I don't have a gang name yet."

"Maybe I'll just call you Mama's Boy."

Squeezy gurgled. Apparently he thought the idea was funny.

Apparently so did I. I gurgled and squealed.

Apparently so did the big baby in the chair behind me. He gurgled even louder. That would be Soggy, Soggy the Load, Squeezy's button man. He was the second most feared baby in North Wood after his older brother Baggy the Load, who still did odd enforcer jobs for the gang when Soggy had too much to handle.

"That sounds good. I like my mom." I thought of her giant milky bosoms. That made me feel hungry, and I felt like crying. I tried to hold it together.

"I heard you might have some good moves, kid. You certainly know how to get attention."

Soggy thought that was hilarious. He cooed and squealed and spat up a half ounce of the white on to his chest. Something smelled foul from his direction. I was pretty sure he was sitting in his own shit. I was starting to think Soggy was your run of the mill, milk-fed infant gangster moron. He couldn't help it. His parents were probably your run of the mill Tall Tree grass-fed adult morons.

"You would be referring to the incident at the bank?" I asked, curling my lip into what I was hoping would look like a smirk.

"Exactly," Squeezy said, puffing on his pacifier for effect. "That was an A1 job you pulled."

That was less than a week ago. Mom had taken me down to the bank to do some transactions. After about a half hour of hanging around in the stroller listening to them bag on about interest rates and

CDs and who-knows-what in what is essentially a flat economy, anyway, I'd decided my wet diaper wasn't drying itself and it was time to eat. I let out a few peeps to shoot across the maternal bow. Unfortunately, by then, mom was halfway through a stack of paperwork and couldn't easily wrap it up. I was gonna let it ride and see if I could just conk out for a while to avoid the discomfort. Mom is cool beans. You have to give her some operating room. But then the manager comes over in his cheap suit and garish tie and starts poking my toes, saying, "has someone got your foot? Has someone got your foot?" over and over again, as if I can't figure out who is holding my frickin' foot from twenty inches away. So now I'm up and annoyed and wet and hungry and feeling a little condescended to, and I can't go to sleep because this guy is poking my toes and asking stupid questions. So I decide to go straight from zero to thermonuclear. I scream and yell and throw my arms and legs so hard I rattle the baby seat. The patrons are looking perturbed. The manager retreats a few paces, but I keep it up. Even mom is looking worried. She's never seen me like this.

Well, mom pushes the stroller back and forth and pulls me out of the baby seat to put me over her shoulder and then tries the bottle she carries around.

I keep rattling like a berserker.

The manager is beside himself now, and the pretty ladies who work the clerk counters have come around to see if they can help. A few of the customers are coming over to see what's what, and a lady with a three year old girl leaves when her daughter breaks down crying because she can't take the stress of watching me wail. All I know is I am making noise and getting a response.

Now comes the haul. After a little while, the manager runs away into the back somewhere and returns with a soft plushy thing shaped like the bank's colorful logo and another toy that rattles when I wave it around.

That's good enough for one day, plus mom needs a break, so I quiet down with my two toys in my hands and pass out.

It was pretty much your ordinary meltdown caper, except that pulling one off at my age was way ahead of schedule. You could say I was one of those early developers.

It wasn't long before I got the call from Squeezy.

"Yeah, that was a class gig you pulled," Squeezy said, agreeing with himself. "A good haul, prime target, and nobody got hurt." He puffed on his pacifier. "I could use a kid like you."

"What do you have in mind?" I asked, stuffing my hand in my mouth. I guess I was getting hungry.

"A big score. This is gonna require finesse."

"Sounds interesting," I said, trying to sound suavely diffident. "Finesse I have." I hated that this was the precise moment I crapped in my diaper.

"We're going to take down the milk load in the refrigerator at Zero Day right after the Breast Feeding Master Class."

I didn't know what to say, so I just waved my arms a lot.

"I know. It's an ambitious plan. But if you don't dream, kid . . . ." He trailed off. "Sometimes you gotta aim big and just go grab it. It can be a heavy burden to be on top." He looked wistful and gazed at his socks.

I was getting the impression Squeezy wasn't altogether the most together baby gangster in history. He was ambitious enough. But his thought process didn't seem very organized. Maybe Mr. Cheeks really did need my help.

"Sounds like a big haul," I said, mostly to keep him on track.

"It is a known fact that the Zero Day Breastfeeding Master Class produces the biggest single volume of fresh white in all of Tall Tree. It's perfect. You got the full production moms three weeks in who are still getting their technique. You have the hyper tiger moms one day out of hospital still spilling colostrum. Colostrum! You know how hard it is to get your hands on colostrum these days? It's so pure, so distilled. The kids crave it, will do almost anything to get their hands on it. All this milk gets collected and bottled in the first half of the class, and then they put it in the fridge during the second half of the class when they talk about baby products they need to buy. There are no guards, no cameras, no alarm system. Only dozens of freshly lactated milk bottles sitting, waiting, begging to be nabbed."

He had raised his chin, affecting the look of a general at war gazing into the distance and the face of destiny.

"Sounds like a huge opportunity."

"It is!" He pounded the sides of his seat. "A huge opportunity. Even bigger than you think. If I can get my hands on the Zero Day load, I will finally have enough power to smash the Poopypants Gang once and for all!"

LITTLE TROUBLE IN TALL TREE

CHAPTER TWO

So there it was. Just weeks out, and I had already found myself in the middle of the ugliest baby gang war in Santa Infanta County. The Poopypants crew ruled the South Wood. Their leader, a particularly fat and loathsome mewler named Harry the Rash, ruled the gang with an iron rattle, having pushed out the other local bosses with an unrelenting brand of intimidation and violence. The word around Story Time was that the Rash was gearing up to come after Squeezy's territory next.

He was apparently already nibbling at the edges. Babies wearing the Rash's bright colors were seen taking more than their share of snacks at the Kids' Zoo on California Ave, and they had begun to muscle in on the northwest corner of the room during Story Time at the JCC, where the shade and breeze were in highest demand. The Kids' Zoo was right on the middle dividing line of Tall Tree, but the JCC was on Cowper Street, already inside North Wood. Squeezy probably thought that if he didn't respond, the other crews would think he had lost it. That explained everything.

Zero Day was deep in the heart of South Wood. A caper there would not only flood Squeezy with power but send a message that no amount of milk was safe anywhere in Tall Tree.

I had to hand it to him. His plan was strategic. Maybe Squeezy was a subtle genius after all. This baby seemed, all at once, to be inscrutable.

LITTLE TROUBLE IN TALL TREE

CHAPTER THREE

I had a few days to contemplate the caper and my new boss's brain.

I was sitting there at Story Time, contemplating, half listening to the lady read a narrative about sheep who get stuck in a jeep and the pigs who help them out of the mud. She's turning the book around after she reads every page so we can see the sheep bounce around in the jeep, and all the babies who didn't get into the first row are squinting because the book is so small the sheep might as well be milk blots and the jeep a weirdly shaped nipple, and the half of my brain that is paying attention is half wondering if this wouldn't be much easier over PowerPoint the way they do it at dad's office. Then I start to tune it out altogether, since what I really think is she should be reading a book about the pigs, who seem so much more generous, personable, and good-humored than the hapless sheep who do nothing but drive into mud and then into trees and then cry for help or try to hide the evidence of their chaos.

I was contemplating all this, plus the caper and my boss's brain, plus the ingredients that somehow make each of my ten fingers taste so delicious, and why they taste so differently delicious one at a time as compared to when I suck on them together, and how the different combinations all have different flavors, and I was close to working out how many combinations of fingers I might be able to stuff in my mouth at once, and I was partly wondering when I could get my own email account, since that seemed to be a pretty popular topic with mom and dad, when she pulled up next to me in her stroller.

She was a knockout. I'd put her at 26 inches tall, big oval pods of blue for eyes, and a monkey patterned onesie that showed off exactly the right amount of décolletage for Story Time. This gal was class. What got me, though, was her bright red hair. Mom's hair is auburn, so I know I'm supposed to have a thing for redheads. I do.

I decided to play it cool. I stuffed both hands into my mouth and waited for her to make the first move.

She turned her head my way and beamed me a smile. She had a beautiful tooth.

"I'm Daisy!" She kicked her feet up in the air and laughed.

"Howdy," I replied. I found myself stretching my arms out her way.

"I'm new in town," she continued.

"Ain't everybody?" I asked, facing forward again and breathing a sigh that hopefully sounded more like boredom than fatigue.

I was pretty sure I had established dominance, but I didn't know what came next in the mating ritual.

"I kinda have a problem," she continued.

"Oh, yeah, what's that?"

"I'm not trying to sound stuck up, but there's a baby who won't leave me alone. I met him here at Story Time a while ago, and now he thinks I'm his girl or something."

"Sounds like one of your lowlife barfer types," I said, leaning forward, hoping she would notice that my hair covered the entire crown of my head.

"Exactly! He's an ugly pug, too, and constantly trying to show off."

"What's his name?"

"I don't even know, and of course I don't ask when I see him, since I think it will just encourage his behavior."

"You mean he never told you when you first met?"

"Uh, maybe he did, but I guess I forgot! Anyway, I see him too often for my taste at Story Time, and he comes over and harasses me. Blech. I'm just wondering if I can sit here and we can pretend we're talking if he shows up."

"Of course we can, dolly," I said, smashing the side of my seat harder than I had intended and startling myself and the baby in front of us as my stroller rocked and rolled forward into him. "But why don't you point him out to me now?"

"I don't see him," she said, craning her neck and swinging it around and around. "Maybe he's not coming today. Sometimes he comes late."

"Can you describe him? Maybe I can take a look, find out more about him for you."

"You can do that for me?"

"I've got some moves." I grabbed my right foot with both hands and stuffed it in my mouth. I'm pretty sure she looked impressed.

"Okay, I'll do my best."

She then offered the most generic, least revealing description of any baby – or of every baby – I'd ever heard. All I could tell from what she told me was that he was pudgy, still wore his baby fat, had a little hair that looked dark or not depending on the lighting, and that he might have some strawberrying or birth marks on his arms or legs or neck. It was impossible to do anything with what she gave me. Either this girl had some aggressive form of early onset Alzheimer's or she was actually a lot more frightened than she had initially let on and was trying to throw me off the track after she sniffed that I was connected to the underworld.

LITTLE TROUBLE IN TALL TREE

CHAPTER FOUR

"It's on for Saturday."

Squeezy sat in his chair, dressed in a black velour jumpsuit. Apparently he liked how soft it was. He rubbed his hands up and down on his belly and gripped the zip-up shirt.

On his desk were a group of fierce looking stuffed dinosaurs. He had arranged them and some wooden blocks to show the layout of the Zero Day Maternity Store. Squeezy himself wore a menacing grimace you might have after three days of hardcore jailbird constipation. A cold shiver ran down my spine, and then the tingle of excitement you get when you first put your hands on a fresh bottle and the nipple is an inch from your lips. This was all getting very real now.

"Here's the outline, fellas," Squeezy continued.

"And ladies." That would be Maggie. She was your classic brazen baby gangster moll. She'd been hardened by spending the first two weeks of her life amid the rat-a-tat squalor of East Tall Tree before her family had relocated across the highway to leafier parts. She was correctly feared. No one uttered a whisper about her palling just a little closer than most with Mr. Cheeks over at the Kids' Zoo Bunny Zone. Maggie was one half of the North End gang's active female roster.

The other half was her best friend Mackenzie. They called her Ninja Spit, which sounded lethal, but I guess you just had to take their word for it. I hadn't seen what they were talking about yet. She was quiet like a ninja, alright, so quiet she might be sitting smack in front of you for a whole bottle without your knowing she was there. But she did not seem threatening. Mostly she drooled. Olympically long, continuous, high-viscosity strands of drool. Pools of drool collected on her clothes. Was Ninja Spit like an inside joke name? I didn't have a complete handle on baby gangster humor.

Anyway, Maggie the Moll wanted the Cheeks to acknowledge that the gang wasn't just fellas any longer.

"Excuse me. Here's the outline, fellas and ladies." Squeezy pointed at his map.

"The Breastfeeding Master Class begins at 11 and ends at 1. All you babies whose moms aren't in the class are gonna have to get to Zero Day for whatever reason by 11:45. At noon exactly, the big blonde lady from Zero Day will emerge from the Easy Lactation Room with an entire tray of the white. This is our motherlode. Each mom has her own bottle with her name on it. The tray is crammed full of 'em. You can tell the ones with colostrum because they're tiny.

"Big blonde lady takes the tray, walks over to the pantry, places the tray down on the floor during the transfer, and one by one places the bottles in the mini-fridge. That's where they stay until 1, when the moms come out and go over to get the bottles with their names on them.

"Careful observation has shown that it takes Blondie five minutes to get everything into the fridge. That gives us a fifty-five minute window to get in, grab the stash, and get out without anyone calling the fuzz."

He leaned forward. The high hat light on the ceiling cast a new and imposing shadow across his massive jowls.

"As soon as Blondie has put the goods in the mini-fridge and left the pantry, we're going to create a huge diversion. Leading the charge on the diversion will be Sammy the Whine. You will take your cue from him."

Sammy the Whine. A good move. He was a legend. The sorest loser and losingest baby card shark in Tall Tree. When he gets going, he makes a five alarm fire sound like a Dream Sheep.

The gang grunted and gurgled their approval. Squeezy raised his hands above his head for silence.

"You know what will happen next. The place will erupt with staff trying to calm us down. Mommies will run around like headless birds. You must throw, maul, slam, and scream about everything you can see or touch.

"Meanwhile, an elite team led by me and Soggy the Load will sneak into the pantry, work the mini-fridge door, and grab the white. We'll stuff it into our rides so no one will be the wiser."

He removed his pacifier and waved it around for emphasis. "I don't have to tell you that this is a precision job, requiring the utmost care and planning. There is no room for error! Our stealth must be maximum! Our kung-fu must be perfect!"

I couldn't help myself. The Cheeks's speech was rousing. I leaned forward in my seat and waved my arms around. I threw up an ounce.

"This is the most important operation in North Wood baby gangland history. Each of you will be part of that history." He waved his arms. "Together, we will seize the biggest load of white – and the biggest ever load of colostrum – that Tall Tree has ever seen. We will use the power this score gives us to smash the Poopypants Gang to smithereens, and then we will unify the North and South Woods for the first time in memory!"

The gang was excited and deeply moved by his charge. I sniffed the growing scent of curdled formula. More than one baby must have thrown up, and several followed suit. The stench became overwhelming. Then one baby gangster started to cry. And another. And another. Then for some reason I felt like crying. Oh brother.

As we sat there, cheering and throwing up and crying, I couldn't help that one part of my brain was telling me something was very, very wrong with this plan.

LITTLE TROUBLE IN TALL TREE

CHAPTER FIVE

Friday came, one day before the big heist, and most of the gang tried to make like they were going about their regular business. The babies showed up at the Kids' Zoo and Story Time and the Johnston Park sandbox like always, and they babbled about sheep in jeeps and sweet potato vs. squash mash to keep their minds off the job and throw the scent in case anyone had leaked farther than his diaper. To an outsider, everything looked normal. But to anyone who knew what he was looking at, the tension was bubbling over. The babies were on edge. Soggy was so jumpy that when his mom laughed at a friend's joke, he knee jerk squeezed his bottle to spray her in self-defense. Sammy the Whine sat around the sandbox sighing, perhaps weighing the heavy burden of his key role in the heist. Even Mackenzie the Ninja Spit drooled more conspicuously and acidically than usual.

I kept crapping out my diaper all day. I must have changed seven diapers before dinner. Most of the craps were huge surprises. I'd be sitting around, playing with mom's keychain, and WHOOSH!, I'd have a huge crap in my diaper. Total surprise, taking me off-guard. I'd sit up, eyes wide open like a deer in headlights wondering if anyone around me was as surprised as I was or had massive surprise craps, too.

Daisy showed up at Story Time. I went over in the afternoon to take my mind off things. Besides, Friday was Very Hungry Caterpillar day, and I like that book. Eric Carle didn't know how to draw for shit, but the man could tell a story. The library lady reads the Caterpillar in English and Spanish at the same time, which makes it more interesting.

I was hanging around the back waiting for the part when the caterpillar ducks into his chrysalis – every baby gangster likes the idea of a chrysalis – a chance to go underground and be reborn as something other than the meal to meal tough nut you are – when I spotted Daisy over by the Food Groups poster. She was talking animatedly to Jamie the Phlegm.

The Phlegm was your run of the mill, blue-blood east coast Congregationalist transplant who was slumming it in gang life while he waited for the turnstile of time to deposit him at Princeton Day School and then Princeton High School and finally Princeton University. He was the kind of baby who would listen in rapture to Very Hungry Caterpillar and then describe it as a "great book." It wasn't his fault he was such a wet diaper. His parents did not let on they had feelings, either. His dad never failed to wear a golf windbreaker and boat shoes to any of the Sunford University football games. He had to be ready for a sudden breakout of WASP sports at any time.

Jamie had signed on to Squeezy's North Wood gang only just before I had. I didn't know what his special skill was. But I could say for sure he was very good looking. Probably already 30 inches tall, he was muscular and broad, with a shock of blonde hair and piercing light blue eyes. Even his ruddy baby cheeks were chiseled in steely outline around their puffiness. He looked like an Autobot.

I confess I was a little jealous when I saw Daisy talking to him so close.

I waved at her. At least I think I waved. It's hard to tell what your limbs do sometimes. Either way she didn't notice. I craned my head to get her attention, but she was deep into it with Jamie. For his part, he didn't seem to mind, but he wasn't all that committed to the conversation. I wondered why. You can never tell with these studmuffin babies when they ignore the women. They're either gonna be gay or those movieland high school quarterbacks who don't heed the girls because they're dripping off tree branches at them. Or maybe the Phlegm had bad hearing and couldn't make out what Daisy was saying.

I decided to try to take my mind off the jealous present by channeling my gurgle chakra. I faced forward in my chair, closed my eyes, and opened my mouth wide in a guttural lion's pose like the one I saw mom do after coming home from the office. I bellowed. It was working. The room stilled around me. I felt myself lighter and airier in my chair. In my outer ear, I could hear a stirring, the crying of babies. I bellowed louder, more deeply from my belly.

It was too much. I convulsed and spat up lunch. I opened my eyes in time to see my projectile white land square on the hairdo of the baby in front of me. She didn't mind, but her mom lost it.

I had crapped my pants again. No wonder I was feeling lighter. The whole business stank.

I drooped into my seat, feeling bad about my fit of jealousy and unsuccessful in my baby yoga. Mom was taking me to all the classes and practicing extra at home right in front of me. All I had to do was pay attention. But I was not on top of my poses. I felt so behind.

The Story Time lady finished the Very Hungry Caterpillar twice through, and then she and her assistant sang a round robin of "Row Your Boat." Then we did some organized cheering.

I was feeling tired and squishy as we started to roll out. My eyelids narrowed to slits as the bobbing of the stroller took over. My brain edged toward the lustful oblivion of giant milk breasts and infinity splashy baths.

"Hi!"

I startled awake. It was a pity. I had been so close to the milkiest bosom of all time, preparing to faceplant into the nipple and engorge myself as my arms and legs cascaded bath water all around my person.

"It's Daisy!" she shrieked and tossed a curl. I felt instinctively that I could have been more put together. My face was buried in the side of my chair, and I was drooling like an infant Niagara Falls.

"Hello, Daisy." I asserted myself. A baby passed by, and I wrinkled my nose at his behind so she would think the foul brew was his.

"It's so good to see you!" she said, reaching an arm out my way. "You look really great."

Really? I didn't think I could look all that good. But I confess it made me feel cool when she said that. I had to burp badly but decided to hold it in if I could.

"Listen," she continued, "have you found out any more about that creep? I keep seeing him everywhere. He always bothers me every time."

Of course I hadn't learned anything more. How do you learn more about a baby who looks like everybody and nobody? A baby gangster cipher. I wanted to reply but couldn't open my mouth or I'd let out belch and pasty formula. The pressure in my gut was building up. I gripped the sides of my stroller and shook my head no. I'm pretty sure I looked like I was writhing in agony.

"Well, okay," she said, "see you later!" and she brushed my elbow on the roll out of the room.

As she rode off, I found myself looking at the goose bumps forming on my arm. Baby butterflies flapped their wings in my stomach. My burp burst through, and I winced at the acrid smell.

"THIS IS YOUR D-DAY"

46   LITTLE TROUBLE IN TALL TREE

CHAPTER SIX

"Tomorrow is your D-Day." Squeezy was declaiming. "Tomorrow is their Waterloo. Tomorrow you will march across your Rubicon and smash the Hun with impunity."

The boss was in fine fettle. He was monologuing for us. Some of it was hard to follow. Baby gang leaders often become philosophical as they grow more prosperous. They place their turf wars in the long line of historical struggles for political supremacy. Most baby gangsters have no idea what they are talking about. But it sounds important, and babies are excitable.

"Tomorrow you will blast the Reds into smithereens! You will carpe diem and decimate the Ostrogoths!"

He went on like that for a while. The gang were getting so inspired they were spitting up en masse. I thought I was more diffident about it but found I was wrapped up enough in the moment that I didn't even pay attention to my rice puffs.

LITTLE TROUBLE IN TALL TREE

CHAPTER SEVEN

I arrived at Zero Day at 11:30, fifteen minutes before I was due. When you're the low baby on the totem pole, it pays to be extra early. They can never fault your work ethic.

I snooped around the hand puppet shelves to mark time and scope out the premises. I had the wrong idea about hand puppets. Here I'd been thinking they were fantastic. They bounce and talk and bite your nose when mom puts her hands into them. I sidled over to a group of lions sitting together as casually as I could and then all of a sudden, I leapt forward at them for a scare. They didn't move a muscle. It turns out that, sitting on the shelves, they don't do anything fun. You need momma's magic. When you're a baby gangster, little by little, your happy delusions get eroded by hard reality.

I held on to the lion shelf with my hands and put a furry foot in my mouth to look inconspicuous. I peered around and took in the room.

Something felt wrong.

There were too many babies milling around. Babies hanging around the rocking chair display. Babies inspecting the Moses baskets. Babies gripping the cardboard boxes containing new model lactation pumps.

Babies I didn't recognize.

I saw our guys, too. There was Sammy the Whine pawing the jars of infant supplements, probably warming up his voice for the big performance. Mackenzie the Ninja Spit was nearby drooling on a Bugaboo stroller. Squeezy himself was across the room, trying to look as if he was absentmindedly munching on a bowl of squishy peas. Jamie the Phlegm was sitting with his back against a wall in the toys section holding a rubber mesh football and getting attention from the girls. Maggie the Moll was repeatedly hitting a single note on a long xylophone over by Musical Play. There was even Soggy the Load hunched over by the Shape Sorter trying to push a square peg into a round hole. That kid is an idiot. But he was there. And I thought I noticed his older brother Baggy trouncing around by the Dutalier Glider section.

But there were others, too. Lots of others. Not anyone I'd seen at the gang meetings. A few I'd seen at Story Time, and a few others at the park by the swing set. But some of these cats were new.

They were hard looking babies, too, with mean faces, baby trenchcoats, and the low-slung, triple load diapers favored by the nastiest crappers in Santa Infanta County. They mewled around the store, snorting and burping acrid gas, not even pretending to show interest in the goods on display. I counted a dozen of them before I lost track.

A shiver went down my spine, and I stuffed the lion's other foot in my mouth.

"You have to help me!"

I jumped and turned to see Daisy only a baby's length away. Sometimes I think my priorities are all turned around. My first thought was whether she'd think it was cooler if I stuffed both lion's feet in my mouth at the same time.

I smiled at her then turned away and then back at her in a knee-jerk real-time flirt. She seemed to scowl at me.

"What's the problem?" I recovered. I tried to make my voice sound deep. I was conscious that Jamie the Phlegm had a pretty deep voice. Maybe that's what women want.

"He's here!"

"He is?"

"Yes!" she blurted. "Yes, he is!"

"Oh." I glanced around. I felt I was still coming up to speed. "Who?"

Daisy's hands flew above her head. "The creep I've been telling you about! The one who keeps bothering me! Don't you listen to anything?"

"Yes, of course," I said. "Naturally, the creep. That much was obvious." Every time I see a redhead, I end up talking like Inspector Clouseau.

"So what are you going to do about it? Can you help me?"

"What do you want me to do?"

"Go over there and confront him and make him stop harassing me!"

I was overcome with nausea and felt like throwing up. I guess I had really fallen for this girl hard.

"Which one is he?"

"There! He's right there!"

I followed the path of her hysteria.

"Are you sure? That's the one?"

"Yes!" she screamed. "I'd remember him anywhere. He's horrible! He just won't leave me alone!"

I felt like someone had suckerpunched me in the gut. She was pointing at Squeezy the Cheeks.

"Berserker!!!!!!!" Just then, a great yell went up from a baby at the back of the room.

"Berskerkeeerrrrr!!!!!" The babies I hadn't recognized – the mean looking ones spread around the room – suddenly threw off their trenchcoats and yelled out in unison.

"Berserker!!!!!!" Again I heard the first baby's voice. I craned my neck and saw, emerging from nearby the Easy Lactation Room door, Harry the Rash, fat and fearsome leader of the Poopypants Gang, raising and shaking his iron rattle with terrible vigor.

What is he doing here? I thought to myself as I snatched my head around to see the action unfolding precipitously before me.

"Berskerkeeerrrrr!!!!!" His henchmen replied. And now they raced as one group toward the Easy Lactation Room door.

I could barely make out what was going on. I looked up at the clock. It seemed like it was probably noon, though I'm much better at telling time on digital than analog.

"Go get him!" Daisy shouted in my ear, starting to wail. "Go get him!" She pointed at Squeezy.

As if on cue, Blondie the Tray – a huge, healthy looking young woman – appeared at the Easy Lactation Room door, carrying a bathtub sized platter of bottles brimming with frothy white. From my vantage point, I could make out a nest of small vials of rich, yellow brew. The colostrum.

Harry the Rash waved his arms wildly in the air. The nasty looking babies hurled themselves toward Blondie all at once. A look of fear saturated her face as she saw a horde of baby gangsters heading her way.

"GO GET HIM!" Daisy blasted my eardrum. She

was near full meltdown mode. I could feel my blood pressure skyrocketing.

I froze. Too much was happening around me. I couldn't follow. I didn't know what to do. I didn't know what was going on.

I looked at Squeezy the Cheeks. He was watching the action intently, not moving a muscle. So were Sammy the Whine, Soggy and Baggy the Load, Maggie the Moll, and the other veterans. Glancing at Jamie the Phlegm, I could see he was agitated; like me, he was frozen in place.

It looked like the Poopypants Gang was about to carry out a massive hit on our score, right in front of our eyes, right under our noses, only minutes before we could execute our own plan. I didn't know if I should hurl myself at them to save the day or fly at Squeezy with a samurai attack and save the honor of the girl. It was all too much to think about it so fast. All the commotion was too exciting. I crapped in my diaper.

"Berserker!!!!" Harry shouted again.

"Berskerkeeerrrrr!!!!!" His gang answered. And now they consummated their assault maneuver. As Blondie the Tray walked, burdened by her heavy load, baby after baby rolled directly into her path. She navigated sprightly first one and then a second and then a third, finding her sure footing each time around the babies' bodies, but they crowded into her way too quickly. She did what any farmed veal maternity store clerk would do and swerved to avoid them. Maternity store clerks have no stomach for carnage. To save the babies, she tripped, and the tray of bottles scattered to the winds.

The baby henchmen followed the goods, scrambling to grab as much of the load as they could. I saw Harry the Rash himself in the middle of the press, giving orders to his men and stacking his own pile of the loot.

At that moment, when all hell was breaking loose on the floor of Zero Day, the loudest, shrillest, most baleful caterwaul ever heard in Tall Tree sailed into the air and over the heads of everyone in the room. It was a tweener's shriek and a fire engine siren and a crack of thunder rolled into one.

We all stopped in our tracks and looked overhead to trace the source of the screaming. It was, of course, Sammy the Whine. He hadn't moved from the infant supplements. He was sitting on the floor, his throat open and head up toward the ceiling like a baby Placido Domingo, his chest puffed out and palms upraised to help him project. It looked like a kind of prayer wail. The shriek penetrated every corner and crevice of your ear and seeped into your bones. It played with your mind. I was so nervous I crapped in my diaper again.

Out of the corner of my eye, I noticed Squeezy the Cheeks and Soggy the Load accelerating their way toward the scattered bottles of milk and colostrum. Then I saw a bunch of other babies move in from every direction. The Poopypants Gang were distracted by Sammy's terrible whine. They didn't notice at first.

"I said GO GET HIM! NOOOWWWW!!!!!!" Daisy slapped me in the face and switched her wailing into sixth gear.

I was overwhelmed. The surprise caper by the South Wood gang, Daisy's tantrum, Sammy the Whine's volcanic voice attack, and even Squeezy's quick thinking clever counter-caper were too much for me to handle. I felt hot and confused, and my diaper was full of fresh doody. I couldn't take it any more, and my inexperience got the better of me.

Without warning, I went thermonuclear.

I threw myself on the floor and banged my fists and feet. I yelled and screamed and mewled. I rolled on my back and then back onto my belly. I threw the lion away and then chased after it to throw it away again. I banged my head on the floor by accident and then raged about the injustice of that. I cried and shouted and then gasped for air to refuel as I ran out of oxygen. Feeling lonely, I crawled my way toward the Easy Lactation Room door to be near the action.

I paused long enough to see the babies with mean faces staring at me. At first I was frightened. These infants could easily have smashed me up pretty badly. But then I realized they were the ones who were scared. Or at least they were confused. I must have looked pretty raw. These were hard babies. No doubt they had seen a lot. But they were looking at me like I had a second head.

But behind and between them, Squeezy and his gang had not stopped moving. They were amidst the fallen bottles now, spread out across the drop zone like tot paratroopers.

And to my surprise, they were deliberately spilling the bottles on the floor.

It didn't take long for Harry and his henchmen to realize what was happening. They wheeled around and fought back to rescue their hoard. But it was too late. The floor was already thick with frothy breast milk, and maneuvering in the muck was hard. Visibility was low.

I scrambled into the fray to save some precious bottles of the white. I grabbed what I could and stuffed it into my pants.

I felt a hand on my shoulder. "No, Mama's Boy. That's not the plan. Spill what you touch. Destroy it all." It was Baggy the Load, Soggy's older brother. He patted me on the back and headed off toward another pile of bottles that needed draining.

Confused, I turned the bottles upside down and watched the fresh milk empty out.

Soon, as quickly as they had launched their assault, the Poopypants henchmen, and Harry with them, dispersed from the battle and out into the street.

LITTLE TROUBLE IN TALL TREE

CHAPTER EIGHT

It was a few days later before I saw Squeezy the Cheeks and the gang. The heat was on after such a big caper, and he didn't want us to call attention to ourselves by convening too quickly.

When I did see Squeezy, he was behind his desk wearing a khaki jump suit. He puffed on a pacifier. Only a few other babies were present. Soggy sat behind me, as usual, and Baggy sat next to him, holding a real metal fork. Maggie was there, and Sammy the Whine was staring at her bright yellow sandals. And I thought I saw one other baby lurking in the shadows, but I couldn't make out who it was.

"I want to tell you I'm sorry, Mama's Boy," he began.

The truth is I had been dreading seeing him since Saturday. I had a feeling he was going to kick me out of the gang as swiftly as he had invited me to join. I had committed a humiliating, amateur hour, freshman mistake, possibly jeopardizing the entire operation. The high intensity events of that half hour had all been too much light and sound for me. The meltdown I'd had should have been avoided. For anyone else, I felt, it would have been avoided.

"You know, boss, I'm kinda relieved," I said quietly.

"Why?"

"I don't know if I'm cut out for this."

Squeezy gurgled. Apparently he thought that was funny.

"Don't know if you're cut out for this." He laughed louder now.

The babies behind me gurgled with him. I thought I heard Soggy slap his knee, though I was sure that if I didn't know what we were laughing about, he didn't know, either.

"No, no, no, Mama's Boy, I think you have the wrong idea. You're perfectly cut out for this!"

"I am?" I brightened.

"Yes! You are terrific. I wanted to apologize for misleading you."

"For what?"

"For misleading you," he said. He removed his pacifier and placed his hands on his belly. "Only the babies in this room knew the real plan. Some time ago, I received intelligence that Harry the Rash was planning on striking the Zero Day motherlode. If he had put that much colostrum and white on the street, the power he would have accumulated could have devastated us. We needed to stop him from getting his hands on that score.

"I knew how I would have handled that heist. In fact, the way I would have handled that heist was pretty much exactly the way I laid it out for you the other day. It would have been elegant. A masterbabystroke. Sublime infant criminality. But the Rash would never be so elegant. He wouldn't know elegant if it crapped on his face.

"No, Rash and the Poopypants know only one thing. They know their berserker attack – a fearsome and effective tool, I have to confess, and most troubling to replicate – and they know recklessness and violence. I understood that, given their tactics, their main opportunity would be the broad daylight frontal assault on Blondie the Tray as she made her way from the Easy Lactation Room to the pantry. That meant two things. The first, we would not have a chance to steal the load our way. And second, because we could not steal the goods our way, we would have to foil their attempt and destroy the load altogether."

I was stunned. I sat where I was, wide-eyed. My eyebrows shot to the top of my forehead. My mouth must have been gaping. After a while, I felt the drool start to seep through my shirt.

"That's amazing, Squeezy." I said, finally. "It's nice of you to apologize, but I guess I don't think you need to do that."

"I'm not finished yet, Mama's Boy," he replied. "I knew that, to pull off our plan, we would have to distract the Poopypants boys long enough to get into the middle of the scattered bottles so we could destroy the white. Harry's crew are nasty, tough South Siders, the worst of the worst. They're veterans, too. They don't spook easily. Some of them have been with the Rash long enough to have fought in the Hummus War.

"You remember that, Baggy?"

Baggy looked up from touching the sharp tines on his fork. "Of course I do."

"Of course you do. Anyway, Mama's Boy, this is one hard gang. How do you distract a gang like that long enough to move in and have the advantage of surprise?"

"I don't know." I felt I was wide-eyed and drooling again.

"With great respect to Sammy the Whine here," Squeezy continued, "even his special talent can only confuse a gang like that for ten or twenty seconds. To make our plan work, I needed at least twice as much time.

"So I heard about your bank caper and how you held down that suppression tantrum for a good long stretch. You created havoc in there. Everybody said. And you got results. Meanwhile, you're littler than the average kid who can create that kind of havoc, which already is a pretty rarefied group of babies. So you put the picture together – a baby your age who can throw down that hard – and I figure even the Poopypants boys will never see it coming. They'll take one look at you losing your noodle and they'll have to keep staring."

I was literally drooling a hole in my shirt. My eyes were drying out because I hadn't blinked in a century. My mouth was open in a perfect circle.

"The only problem was how to set you off so you'd have a genuine, pin the needle meltdown. The way I heard it is that you were at the bank and one thing after another got on your nerves until finally the man gets in your face and then into your private headspace and breaks the camel's back. That's when you lost it." Squeezy looked at me square in the eyes and smiled. "Listen, kid, don't feel bad. It happens to babies your age.

"To pull off the Zero Day job, I had to create conditions to make you feel overwhelmed at exactly the right moment. I had to measure out the correct balance of confusion, noise, and multiple simultaneous events to push you over the edge so you would activate – what do you call it – your thermonuclear response.

"For this kind of delicate job, I had to call on one of the most talented members of the North Wood Gang. You remember Daisy."

I wheeled around toward the shadows as Daisy emerged to show her face. She was smiling warmly.

"Hi!" she said brightly. "Good to see you. Sorry we had to meet like that."

I was pretty sure I was speechless. I kept shutting and opening my mouth, but nothing was coming out. Something about her looked different, and I screwed up my eyes to see what it was.

"You're right," she said. "I'm not naturally a redhead. I had to wear the wig because we knew your mom's hair is auburn, and we didn't have any room for error. We had to increase our chances by playing the numbers."

I wanted to crap or stretch my arms in disbelief, but I couldn't. I was reeling.

"Mama's Boy," Squeezy continued. "I wanted to apologize for misleading you. I also wanted to say that we couldn't have done it without you, and we're all very proud of you. I am proud of you. All of North Wood is proud of you."

I felt myself beaming. It's impressive what some praise can make you feel. After that they were all back slaps and milk cocktails for the rest of the afternoon. When I presented the tiny bottles of colostrum I had managed to secret away in my pants during the height of the battle, they roared with approval. I wanted very much to talk with Daisy, redhead or not, to see if I had imagined the whole thing, but I didn't. Maybe I didn't have an opportunity to speak with her privately. Or maybe I was too shy. Or maybe I had learned enough new stuff for one afternoon as it was. Sometimes you have to save some for later.

LITTLE TROUBLE IN TALL TREE

CHAPTER NINE

A few days went by, and I was sitting in Johnston Park, pounding the sandbox with my plastic shovel and watching the dappled sunlight make shifting patterns on my pants and on the castle the big kids were making a few feet away. The big kids know how to make the greatest stuff.

I had a lot to think about. Squeezy the Cheeks was pretty much a baby gangster genius. His maneuvers, his subtlety, his supple planning: they were all so mysteriously integrated, intelligently refined. They required serious contemplation. At the same time, I couldn't help but think that somehow there was a frailty there, an unevenness, a gap in his abilities that necessitated assistance from a baby like me. I felt, in some way that I could not yet describe, that I could be of great help to him.

It was then that Baggy the Load came over and crouched next to my spot in the sandbox.

"How you been?" he asked.

"Good. How about you?" I waved around my shovel so he would notice. It was a terrific shovel.

"We got another caper coming up," he said. "A big one. And Squeezy has another special role for you."

"Oh, really?" I was skeptical. I felt I might be the used low totem guinea pig again.

"Yes. But this time we need you to be the teacher. You know that kid Jamie the Phlegm?"

"Yes." I intended to sound diffident and shoveled the sand a little to show that I was.

"Well, he's not really getting it. He's not coming up to speed quickly enough. We need you to show him the ropes. You up for it?"

I beamed with pride and a baby's breath of triumph.

"Of course I am."